Of Mice and Men

JOHN STEINBECK

Level 2

Retold by Kevin Hinkle

Series Editors: Andy Hopkins and Jocelyn Potter

Pearson Education Limited

Edinburgh Gate, Harlow,
Essex CM20 2JE, England
and Associated Companies throughout the world.

ISBN: 978-1-4058-5536-5

First published in the UK by William Heinemann Ltd 1937
First published by Penguin Books 2001
This edition published 2008

1 3 5 7 9 10 8 6 4 2

Original copyright © John Steinbeck 1937
Text copyright © Penguin Books Ltd 2001
This edition copyright © Pearson Education Ltd 2008

Typeset by Graphicraft Ltd, Hong Kong
Set in 11/14pt Bembo
Printed in China
SWTC/01

Published by Pearson Education Ltd in association with
Penguin Books Ltd, both companies being subsidiaries of Pearson Plc

For a complete list of the titles available in the Penguin Readers series please write to your local
Pearson Longman office or to: Penguin Readers Marketing Department, Pearson Education,
Edinburgh Gate, Harlow, Essex CM20 2JE, England.

Contents

Introduction

"And you won't do any bad things?" George demanded. "Do you remember Weed?"

"What happened in Weed, George? I don't remember."

"You forgot that, too? There was trouble in Weed, Lennie."

"I remember," Lennie said happily. "They chased us out of town."

Lennie Small is a big man. He is friendly, and he loves animals and soft things. But Lennie is not very intelligent and he is too strong. He gets scared easily and he often hurts things by accident. George Milton is Lennie's best friend. He is smarter than Lennie, so he tries to help his friend.

George and Lennie work on farms around the country. But they have a plan for the future. They want to buy a farm and have animals and vegetables. But, first, they have to get some money. And Lennie has to stay out of trouble.

John Steinbeck was born in Salinas, California, in 1902. He had many different jobs before he wrote his first book, *Cup of Gold* (1929), and he learned about the lives of different people. His most famous book is *The Grapes of Wrath*, about farm workers in California. Other books by Steinbeck are *The Pearl*, *East of Eden*, and *The Red Pony*. These four books are all Penguin Readers. Most of the people in these stories are not rich or famous. They have hard and usually unhappy lives. Steinbeck understood them and we learn to understand them, too.

Steinbeck's books made him famous around the world and many of them are also famous movies. He was one of the greatest American writers of all time. He died in 1968.

It was early evening in late summer when two men walked down to the river.

Chapter 1   By the Pool

Near the town of Soledad, the Salinas River runs next to some small mountains. The river is full and green and the water is warm from the strong sun. Across the river from the mountains is a line of tall trees and in the trees is a small pool. Farm dogs, rabbits, and other animals run through the trees, and young boys swim in the warm water on summer afternoons.

It was early evening in late summer when two men walked down to the river. They wore heavy blue pants and coats, and large black hats. They put big black bags down on the ground near the water. The day was hot and the men were tired.

One man was small with a dark face and quick eyes. His arms and legs were thin. He saw everything around him. The other man looked very different. He was tall and wide and his walk was slow and heavy. He usually followed the smaller man.

The bigger man was very thirsty so he started to drink from the green pool. He drank and drank.

"Stop it, Lennie," the other man said. But Lennie drank again. "You'll get sick. Remember yesterday."

Lennie slowly put his head under the water. Then he sat up. The water ran down his back.

"That's good. Drink some, George. Have a good, big drink." He smiled happily.

"The water doesn't look good," George said. "It looks dirty." He sat next to the pool and drank water from his hand. "OK. It's not bad," George said. "But you have to be careful when it's not moving."

George washed his face with his hands. Then he put his hat on his head and sat down near the river. Lennie looked at him. Then he pulled his hat down over his eyes, too.

"Give it to me, Lennie."

"George?" Lennie said.

"What do you want?"

"Where are we going, George?"

"You forgot?"

"I forgot. I tried, but I forgot," Lennie answered.

"OK. OK. I'll tell you again," George said. "I have to repeat everything and then you forget again."

"I remember the rabbits, George."

"Forget the rabbits, Lennie! You only remember the rabbits! Rabbits! Now listen to me. I don't want any trouble this time. Do you remember Howard Street?"

Lennie smiled excitedly. "I remember some girls."

"Do you remember the work cards?" asked George.

"Yes, George. I remember them now." He put his hand in his coat. "George, I don't have mine. I lost it."

"No, you didn't lose it," George said. "Do you think I'm crazy? *I* have your work card."

Lennie put his hand into his coat again and pulled something out.

"What did you take from your coat?" George demanded.

"Nothing. I don't have anything in my coat."

"I know you don't now," George said. "What do you have in your hand?"

"Nothing, George."

"Give it to me, Lennie."

"It's only a mouse, George."

"A mouse?"

"Yes. A dead mouse, George. I found it."

"Give it to me," George repeated.

"No, George. It's mine. I found it," Lennie answered.

"Give it here. Now!"

Lennie slowly gave the mouse to George and George threw it

across the pool into the trees. "Why do you want a dead mouse?"

"I like petting it with my fingers," Lennie said.

"You can't pet dead mice when you're with me," George said. "Where are we going, Lennie? Do you remember?"

"I forgot again," Lennie said.

"What's wrong with you, Lennie?" George demanded. "We're going to work on a farm."

"We're going to work on a farm," Lennie repeated. "I remember. Where is the farm, George?"

"It's very near here. We're going to talk to the boss. Listen to me carefully, Lennie! I'll give him the work cards, but don't say a word. Do you understand? Stand there and be quiet. You're a good worker, but you're crazy. Be quiet so we can get the job."

"OK, George. I'll be quiet. I understand."

"What will you say to the boss?" George asked.

"I ... I ..." Lennie thought for a minute. "I won't say anything. I won't say anything." He repeated the words quietly. "I won't say anything. I won't say anything. I won't say anything." Then he said to George, "I'll remember."

"OK," said George. "And you won't do any bad things?" he demanded. "Do you remember Weed?"

"What happened in Weed, George? I don't remember."

"You forgot that, too? There was trouble in Weed, Lennie."

"I remember," Lennie said happily. "They chased us out of town."

"Chased us out of town?" George repeated. "We ran away because they wanted to hurt us. They looked for us, but they didn't find us."

"I didn't forget that." Lennie laughed loudly.

Chapter 2   The Fat of the Land

Night came quickly. The sky was almost dark now. George sat down and put his hands behind his head. Lennie watched him. Then he put his hands behind his head, too.

"You're a lot of trouble," George said. "I'd like a nice easy life and maybe a girl, but I have to stay with you."

Lennie was quiet for a minute. "We're going to work on a farm?" he asked.

"Yes, that's right," George said. "But we're going to sleep here tonight."

"I'm hungry. Are we going to the farm for dinner? I want to eat."

"Tonight we're going to stay right here," George answered.

"Aren't we going to eat?"

"Of course. Find some wood and we'll make a fire. I have three cans of food in my bag."

Lennie walked into the trees. When he came back, he didn't have much wood.

George said, "OK. Give me that mouse."

"What mouse? I don't have a mouse."

"Give me that mouse right now," George demanded. He waited a minute. "Are you going to give me that mouse or do I have to hit you?"

Lennie put his hand slowly in his coat. "It's *my* mouse. I found it by the road. I didn't do anything bad. It wasn't anybody's mouse. I only petted it."

George threw the mouse into the dark woods. Then he sat by the pool and washed his hands. Lennie started to cry.

"Don't cry, Lennie. You're a man."

"I want another mouse," Lennie said. "I like to pet them."

"Maybe you can have a mouse later," George said. "Let's eat

now, Lennie. There's food for four men and it's good and hot."

"I want ketchup, George."

"We don't *have* any ketchup," George shouted angrily. "You know that we don't have ketchup. Why did you ask for ketchup? Sometimes I'd like to live alone and stay on one farm. But no! I have to take you with me. You're crazy and you always make trouble for me. I'm tired of it!"

Lennie looked down at the ground. "George," he said.

George didn't answer.

"George," Lennie repeated.

"What do you want?" George asked.

"I don't want any ketchup," Lennie said. "I don't want it. I'm sorry. I'll leave, George. I'll go away and leave you. I'll leave you alone, George."

"No, Lennie. Of course, you'll stay with me," George said sadly. "You're my friend and you can't live alone."

Lennie looked at his friend. "Tell me, George."

"Tell you what?"

"Tell me about the farm and the animals."

"You're crazy for that farm," George said. "OK. A lot of men work hard on farms. They don't have a family and they move from place to place. They don't have a future. But we're different. We're friends and we have a plan."

"And you help me and I help you," Lennie laughed excitedly.

"You know the story, so *you* tell it," George said.

"No, *you* tell it, George. I forget some of it."

"We're going to buy a little house with some land. We'll have rabbits and chickens . . ."

"*And we'll live off the fat of the land*," Lennie shouted happily.

"Yes," George answered. "We'll live off the fat of the land."

"We'll have rabbits and chickens . . ."

Chapter 3   In the Bunkhouse

The next day, George and Lennie arrived at the farm in the middle of the morning and took their bags to the bunkhouse. There were eight beds in the long room. George put his clothes on a bed and his shoes on the floor. Lennie put his bag down on the floor next to a different bed.

A little later, a short fat man came into the bunkhouse. "Are you the new men?" he asked. "Where were you this morning?"

"The bus left us 15 kilometers away," George answered.

"What's your name?" the man asked.

"George Milton."

"And what's yours?"

"His name's Lennie Small," George said.

"Where did you work before now?" the boss asked.

"Near Weed," George answered.

"You, too?" The boss looked at Lennie.

"Yes. Him, too," George said.

"He doesn't talk much?"

"No, he doesn't, but he's a really hard worker."

"I'm as strong as a horse," Lennie said.

George looked angrily at Lennie, and Lennie looked down at the floor.

"So what can you do, Small?" the boss demanded.

Lennie looked at George.

"He can do everything," George answered.

"Why are you speaking for him?" the boss asked.

"Because he's a little slow in the head," George said. "But he's always the best worker because he's very strong."

The boss looked at George and Lennie. "What are you doing to him?" he asked George. "Do you take his money?"

"Of course not," George answered. "He's a friend."

George looked angrily at Lennie, and Lennie looked down at the floor.

"I'm going to watch you," the boss said. "So be careful." He turned and walked out of the room.

George turned to Lennie. "Why did you speak?" he demanded.

"I forgot, George," Lennie said.

"Yes, you forgot. You always forget. And now he's going to watch us. Don't talk to anybody, Lennie. Remember that!"

A short time later, a thin angry young man with brown eyes came into the bunkhouse.

"Is my father here?" he asked.

"No. Only me and Lennie," George answered.

"Are you the new men?"

"Yes, we are," George said.

"Doesn't the big man talk?"

"Maybe he doesn't want to talk."

"But I want to talk to him. You'll talk to me next time, big man," the young man said angrily. Then he walked out of the bunkhouse.

George watched him go. "What's wrong with him?" George said. "Why's he angry? Lennie didn't do anything."

An old man stood in the doorway. Candy didn't have many friends on the farm, but he knew all of the men very well.

"Curley's the boss's son," he said. "He's a little man so he hates big, strong men. He's dangerous—he always wants to fight."

"Curley's a bastard," George said. "Lennie wants to work, not fight."

"He's the boss's son," the old man repeated. "He can do anything. He's worse now because he married a pretty little woman. She lives in the boss's house and she really likes men."

"We don't know her and we don't want trouble," George said.

The old man walked out through the door again and then turned around. "I have to leave now, but the men will be back

"You'll talk to me next time, big man."

from work in a short time. You won't say anything to Curley about our talk?"

George understood. Curley was a dangerous man.

"Lennie, I'm scared," he said. "You're going to have a problem with Curley. I know it. One day he's going to hit you."

"I don't want a problem with Curley," Lennie said. "Will he really hit me?"

"Stay away from him," George said. "Never talk to him."

"I won't say a word, George," Lennie said.

"What will you do?" George asked.

"When?"

"When there's a problem."

"I don't know," Lennie answered.

"Do you remember last night by the river?" George asked. "Go there. Wait for me in the woods."

"Wait for you in the woods," Lennie said. "OK, George."

Chapter 4   A Dangerous Woman

Suddenly, there was a noise at the bunkhouse door. George and Lennie looked up. A pretty woman stood there in a short dress and red shoes.

"I'm looking for Curley," she said. Lennie's eyes moved slowly over the woman's beautiful body. "Did you arrive today?" she asked.

"Yes," George said. He didn't want to talk to her.

"Sometimes Curley's in here," she said.

"He's not here now," George said.

"I'll find him. Maybe he's outside." She smiled and walked out of the bunkhouse.

"She's a wild woman," George said. "A strange kind of wife. We have to be careful."

"I'm looking for Curley."

"She's pretty," Lennie said. "I like her."

"Don't be crazy, Lennie," George said. "Don't look at her and don't talk to her. She's a dangerous woman and she's Curley's wife. Stay away from her."

"I didn't do anything, George."

"Yes, you did. You looked at her legs," George said.

"I didn't mean anything. I don't like this place," Lennie cried unhappily. "I want to leave here. Let's go to a different farm, George."

"We have to stay," answered George. "We'll make some money and then we'll leave."

"Let's go right now," Lennie said.

"We can't. We have to make some money. Be quiet now. The other men are coming."

A tall man walked into the bunkhouse. He had black hair and carried a large hat. He wore blue jeans and a short coat. Slim was the best worker on the farm. He spoke slowly and he was very smart.

"Fine weather today," he said. He smiled at George and Lennie. "Are you the new men?"

"Yes, we arrived this morning," George answered.

"My name's Slim. I hope you work with me."

"I'm not great," George said. "But that big man there is very strong. He's a really good worker."

A strong man with a large stomach walked in.

"These men arrived this morning," Slim said to him.

"Hi," the other man said. "My name's Carlson. I work with Slim and the other men."

"I'm George Milton and this is Lennie Small," answered George.

"He isn't very small," Carlson said. "*Not* small." He laughed loudly and turned to Slim. "Slim, how's your dog?"

"She's fine. She had nine puppies last night. I killed four of them because she can't feed them all."

"What will you do with the other puppies?" Carlson asked.

"I don't know. First, the mother has to feed them for four or five weeks."

From across the yard, the men heard sounds from the dining room. "It's time for dinner," Slim said. "Let's eat."

Chapter 5   A Problem in Weed

It was almost dark when George and Slim walked back to the bunkhouse after work that afternoon. Slim sat down on a box and George stood near him.

"Thank you, Slim," George said. "Lennie really loves dogs."

"It wasn't anything," Slim answered. "I didn't want to kill them."

George sat down. "Lennie's very happy," George said. "He'll want to sleep with the puppy tonight."

"You were right about Lennie, George. He isn't very smart, but he's a hard worker. He's the strongest man here."

"He can't think, but he listens to you," George said.

"Why do you always work at the same farm? It's strange," Slim said.

"It's not strange," George said. "I help him because I knew his Aunt Clara. His Aunt Clara died, so Lennie came with me. He can't live alone."

"He's a nice man," Slim said.

"I don't have any family," George said. "Lennie and I are friends. We have a good time. Of course, Lennie makes trouble sometimes because he's not smart. He had a problem in Weed—"

"What do you mean?" Slim asked. "What did he do?"

"You were right about Lennie, George."

"You won't tell?" George asked.

"Of course not."

"Lennie saw a girl in a red dress in Weed. He liked the red dress, so he touched it. He likes to touch soft, pretty things. The girl shouted because she was scared. He's very strong, but he didn't hurt her. He only wanted to feel her dress. But the men in Weed were very angry. We had to leave town very fast."

George finished the story and Lennie came into the bunkhouse. He walked to his bed and sat down. Then he turned his face to the wall. George put down his cards slowly.

"Lennie," he said loudly.

"What do you want, George?"

"You can't have that dog here."

"What dog, George?" Lennie asked.

George walked over to Lennie and took the puppy from the big man's arms.

"Give him to me," Lennie said.

"No," George shouted. "You take this puppy to his mother. He was only born last night. Do you want to kill him?"

"Give him to me, George. I'll take him back. I don't want to hurt him. I only wanted to pet him."

"OK. Take him back now or he'll die," George said.

Lennie carried the dog out of the bunkhouse.

"He's a little boy on the inside," Slim said.

"Yes," George answered. "But he's very strong on the outside."

Chapter 6   The Farm

When Lennie came back without the dog, only George and Candy were in the bunkhouse. Each day, Candy cleaned the bunkhouse and did other small jobs around the farm. He

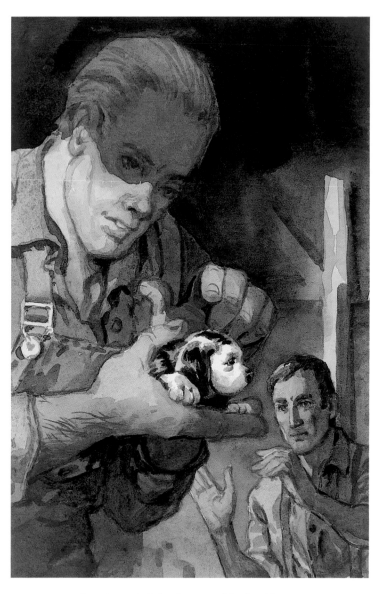

Lennie carried the dog out of the bunkhouse.

didn't do heavy work because he couldn't use his right hand.

"George, when will we have our farm?" Lennie asked.

"I don't know," George said. "First, we have to have some money."

"Tell me about the place, George."

"I told you last night."

"Tell me again, George."

"It's a big farm," George began. "It has a large house with a nice kitchen. There are a lot of fruit trees. And rabbits. We'll have a lot of rabbits. We'll eat meat every night and we'll catch fish every day. We'll cook a chicken for lunch on the weekend. We'll have milk for breakfast, and cream and butter."

"Will we have a good life, George?" Lennie asked.

"Yes, Lennie," George answered. "We'll have vegetables, too. Our table will be full of food. The land will give us everything."

"We'll live off the fat of the land," Lennie said quietly.

"Yes, we'll live off the fat of the land. We'll be happy and we won't run around the country. We won't work too hard, only six or seven hours a day."

George looked happily at the wall over Lennie's head. "We'll have a dog and some cats. Friends can visit us." George wanted to be free. He hoped for a beautiful farm.

"Where is this place?" the old man asked.

"I'm not telling you," George answered.

"That's OK," Candy said. "How much does it cost?" he asked.

George didn't want to answer, but he did. "It's not very expensive. I can buy it for $600. The people have to get some money. Why do you ask, Candy? This plan's for Lennie and me."

"I can't do a lot of work," Candy said. "I had an accident here on this farm and hurt my hand. But they paid me $250. I have fifty dollars more in the bank. That's $300. I'll get another fifty at the end of the month. I can help you. I can give you $350 for the farm. I can't do much work, but I can cook. Can I do that?"

"I'll have to think about it. Lennie and I made this plan for us," George said.

"Do you have any money?" Candy asked. "Maybe we can buy the land now."

"We only have $10," George answered. He thought for a minute. "Lennie and I will work for a month. We'll make $100. That's $450 with your money. I think we can buy the farm for $450. You and Lennie can move in and sell eggs. I can get a job for two or three months. Then we'll have more money."

The three men were quiet. Each man thought about the farm. It really was possible.

"I think we can do it," George said happily. "I think we can do it."

Candy sat on his bed. "I can't stay here. They don't want me here. I'll have to leave and I won't have a place. I want to help you so you'll help me. Take my money and give me a job."

"We'll do it," George said. "We'll buy that old place and make a nice clean home."

The three men thought about the future.

Chapter 7   Trouble with Curley

About an hour later, some of the workers sat in the bunkhouse. Whit, the youngest worker on the farm, played cards with George. Lennie watched the game, and, next to him, Carlson cleaned his gun. Candy sat on his bed with his face to the wall.

Whit asked George, "Did you see the girl, today?"

"What girl are you talking about?" George asked.

"Curley's new wife."

"Yes, I saw her," George said.

"I want to help you so you'll help me."

"She's dangerous," Whit said. "She looks at every man on the farm. She can't stay away from us."

"She's going to make trouble. Curley has a big problem with her," George said. "A farm is no place for a girl."

Whit said, "But town is a good place for girls. I have a great idea. Come with us to town tomorrow night. There are some pretty girls there."

"What happens?" George asked.

"We go to old Susy's bar. It's a nice place, and the girls are clean."

"How much does it cost?"

"It's only two and a half dollars," Whit answered. "You can sit in a chair and have two or three drinks. Or you can have a girl."

"Maybe we'll go," George said. "But Lennie and I don't want to give away all our money."

"A man has to have a good time sometimes," Whit said.

When Whit was quiet, Carlson spoke. "Did Curley come in here?" he asked.

"No," Whit answered. "Why? Is there something wrong with him?"

"There's nothing new wrong with him. I saw him outside earlier. You know he's always looking for his wife."

Suddenly, the door to the bunkhouse opened and Curley ran in.

"Is my wife here?" he demanded.

"She isn't here," Whit answered.

Curley looked angrily around the room. "Where's Slim?"

"He's outside with one of the horses. The horse is sick," Whit said.

Curley didn't say another word. He jumped out the door and closed it loudly behind him.

Whit jumped out of his chair, too, and said, "Let's go. I want to see this. Curley's looking for a fight. He's a good fighter, but Slim's stronger."

"Does he really think Slim's with his wife?" George asked.

"Yes, he does," Whit answered. "Of course, Slim isn't with her. I don't *think* he is. But I want to watch."

"I'm staying here," George said. "Lennie and I want to make some money. We don't want any trouble."

Whit and Carlson left the bunkhouse, but Lennie and George stayed inside with Candy.

"What are you thinking about, Lennie?" George asked.

"Nothing, George. I didn't do anything," Lennie answered.

"Did you see Slim outside with the horses when you took the dog back?"

"Yes, he was there."

"Was the girl there?"

"No, George. I didn't see her."

"Good," George said. "There won't be a fight tonight. Stay away from fights, Lennie."

"I don't want trouble, George," Lennie said. "I don't like fighting."

Five minutes later, they heard noises from outside. George said quickly, "Don't tell anybody about our plan. It's only for us. They won't like our plan and they'll want to stop us."

"OK," Lennie and Candy said.

"Don't tell anybody," George repeated.

Suddenly, the door opened. Slim walked in quickly. Curley, Whit, and Carlson followed him. Slim didn't look happy.

"I didn't mean anything, Slim," Curley said. "It was only a question."

"And I don't like your questions. I'm not interested in your wife," Slim said angrily.

"Stay away from us," Carlson told Curley. "Stay home with your wife."

"I'm not talking to you, Carlson," Curley said. "Do you want a fight?"

"I'm not afraid of you, Curley. Fight me, then. You'll be sorry."

"Yeah, Curley. You're a stupid bastard," Candy said.

Curley looked around the room angrily. His eyes stopped on Lennie. Lennie had a smile on his face because he was happy about their farm.

"Why are you laughing, you big, stupid animal?" Curley demanded. Lennie didn't understand. "I asked you a question," Curley shouted.

Lennie looked at George. He stood up and moved away.

Suddenly, Curley jumped across the room and hit Lennie in the face. He cut Lennie's nose.

The big man cried out loudly. "George," he cried. "George, help me."

"Hit him, Lennie," George shouted. "Hit him!"

"Stop it! Stop it!" Lennie cried, but Curley hit Lennie in the stomach.

"Hit him!" George repeated.

Then Lennie put his big hand around Curley's small hand and started to crush it. Curley fell to the floor.

George ran across the room quickly. "Stop, Lennie," he shouted.

But Lennie didn't stop. George hit Lennie's face again and again, but Lennie didn't stop.

Curley's face was white and he cried like a baby.

"Slim, help me," George said.

Suddenly, Lennie took his hand away. He sat down by the wall. "I didn't want to do it, George," he cried. "You said, 'Hit him!'" he cried.

Slim looked at Curley's hand. "We have to get a doctor. Lennie broke all of Curley's fingers."

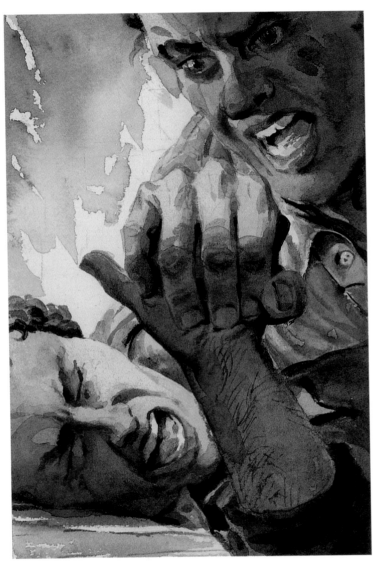

Lennie put his big hand around Curley's small hand and started to crush it.

"I didn't want to hurt him," Lennie said.

"Lennie was afraid," George said. "It's OK, Lennie. You had to fight him."

Chapter 8   Friends

The next evening, Lennie went to visit his puppy. He saw a light in a room next to the dog's home. He walked into the doorway and looked inside.

"What do you want? This is *my* room and I don't want you here," Crooks said. Crooks was the only black worker on the farm, and he lived away from the other men. "I can't come into your room and I don't want you in mine."

"I wanted to see my puppy," Lennie said.

"Go and see it then," Crooks said. "I'm not stopping you."

"Slim says I can't pet the dog," Lennie said. "The mother won't like it." He smiled at Crooks. He wanted to be his friend. "I saw your light. The other men are in town. Only Candy's in the bunkhouse. He's planning our farm."

"You're crazy," Crooks said. "You won't have a farm."

"Yes, we will. George says we will," Lennie answered.

Crooks spoke to Lennie quietly, so nobody outside could hear. "Maybe George won't come back tonight. What will you do, Lennie?"

"He'll come back," Lennie answered. "He always comes back. He won't leave me. Will he?"

"Maybe he'll have an accident. You never know."

"No, George is always careful," Lennie said. "Why are you saying this? George isn't going to have an accident." The big man started to get angry.

"I'll tell you something. They'll hurt you because you're

stupid. When George isn't here, they'll hit you like a dog. Maybe they'll kill you," Crooks said.

Lennie walked angrily across the room.

"Who hurt George?" he demanded. His face was very red. Suddenly, Crooks was afraid of him.

"Nobody hurt George," he said. "He's OK. He'll come back."

"So why are you saying that?" Lennie asked. "George is my friend. He helps me. Don't say bad things about him."

"Sit down, Lennie. Don't be scared. George'll come back. He always does. But, now maybe you can understand *my* life. I'm black and I can't go into the bunkhouse. I have nobody. I'm always out here, and I don't have any friends. I play cards alone in my room. I don't have any friends," he said again sadly.

"George is going to come back," Lennie repeated. "He won't leave me."

"I remember when I was young," Crooks said. "My father had a farm. I had two brothers and they were always there. We slept in the same room, in the same bed. We had fruit and vegetables and chickens—white chickens."

Lennie liked stories about animals, so he started to smile. "George says we'll have rabbits," he told Crooks.

"You're crazy," Crooks said. "Every man here thinks about land. Nobody gets any land. It's all in their heads."

Chapter 9   A Dangerous Game

They heard the sound of a horse outside. "Somebody's out there," Crooks said. "Maybe it's Slim. Is that you, Slim?" he called.

"Slim went into town," Candy shouted into the room. "Is Lennie in there?"

"Are you talking about the big man?" Crooks asked. "He's here."

Candy stood by the door, but he didn't come into the room. "I'm thinking about the animals for the farm, Lennie."

"You can come in," Crooks said. "It's OK. Everybody's coming in here now."

Candy walked slowly in. "You have a nice little place here. This is my first time in this room," he said.

"White men don't come into black men's rooms," Crooks said. "Only Slim and the boss come in here."

"I'm working on the plan for our farm," Candy told Lennie. "George says I can get some animals."

"But I'll feed them," Lennie said happily.

"You're crazy. There isn't going to be a farm. Every man tells the same story. It's all talk," Crooks said.

"George says we're going to do it," Candy said. "We have the money now."

"Yes?" Crooks said. "And where's George now? He's in town. He's paying for women and maybe he's paying with your money. Every man here has land in his head, but it never happens."

"Of course, everybody wants land," Candy said. "We want to live on *our* farm, not the boss's farm. We're going to do it, too. George doesn't have the money in town. The money's in a bank. Me and George and Lennie, we're going to do it. We're going to have dogs and rabbits and chickens and maybe a horse. We're going to have vegetables and fruit."

"Is Curley here?" The men's heads turned to the door. Curley's wife stood there. Her eyes moved around the room.

"So they left the weak men here," she said. "I know the other men are in town."

Lennie watched her. Crooks and Candy looked away.

"You men are funny. You won't talk to me. Are you scared?" She moved her hands down her body to the tops of her legs. Lennie watched her with an open mouth.

"You men are funny. You won't talk to me."

"Go back to the house," Candy said. "We don't want trouble from you."

"I want to talk to somebody," Curley's wife said. "Do you think I like being in that house alone?"

"Get out of here," Candy shouted. "We don't want you here. We don't want to be here. We have a farm with animals and fruit trees and everything. We have some land and we can go to it any time."

Curley's wife laughed at him. "You're a stupid old man. You don't have anything and you're nobody."

"We can't talk to you. We don't have time to talk to you," Candy said. "Go away. Curley doesn't want his wife out here with the men."

The woman looked at each man. She looked at Lennie. "What happened to your face?" she demanded.

"Who—me?" asked Lennie.

"Yes, you."

Lennie looked at Candy for help. Candy didn't speak, so Lennie looked down at the ground. "Curley hurt his hand on a machine," he said.

"A machine? Is that it?" she laughed. "OK, Machine. I'll talk to you later. I like machines."

"Leave him alone," Candy said to her. "I'll tell George about you. You can't talk to Lennie."

"I can talk to anybody," she said.

"I want George," Lennie said. "Where's George?"

"It's OK, Lennie," Candy said. "I can hear the men now. They'll be here in a minute." He turned to Curley's wife. "Go away now and I won't tell Curley."

"Sometimes *I* want to hurt him, too," she said to Lennie. Then she walked out of the room.

"Get out of here," Candy shouted.

Chapter 10   Accidents

The next day was Sunday. In the afternoon, the men played games and laughed outside the bunkhouse.

Only Lennie was inside in one of the farm buildings. He sat on the ground and looked at the dead puppy in his hands.

"Why did you die?" he asked the puppy. "You're bigger than a mouse. I didn't pet you hard." He looked into its face. "Now George will be angry with me." Lennie put the dog down on the ground. "Maybe George won't see it," he thought. He petted the dog's head sadly. "But he'll know. George always knows."

Suddenly, Lennie was angry. "I hate you! Why did you die?" He threw the dead dog across the room. Then he turned his back. "George will be angry. Now I can't feed the animals on our farm." Lennie walked across the room and took the puppy in his large hands. He started to pet it again.

Curley's wife came into the room very quietly. Lennie looked up and saw her.

"What do you have there, big boy?" she asked.

"I can't talk to you," Lennie answered. "George told me."

"Don't listen to George," she said. "He's afraid of Curley, but that's not a problem. You can break Curley's other hand."

"I won't talk to you," Lennie said.

"Why can't I talk to you?" she asked. "I'm always alone. Please talk to me."

"I can't," Lennie answered. "I'll get in trouble."

"What's in your hand?" she asked Lennie. Lennie opened his hand.

"My dog," he said sadly.

"He's dead!" she cried.

"He was little," Lennie said. "I killed him, but it was an accident."

"Why did you die?"

"You can get another dog."

"I can't feed the animals on our farm now," Lennie said. "I want to feed them, but I killed my dog."

Curley's wife sat next to him.

"George says I can't talk to you," Lennie said.

"I won't hurt you," she said. "I won't tell my husband. I don't like him. He's not a nice man. I wanted to be in the movies, but I married Curley. Now he follows me everywhere, so I can't do anything. I can't live my life."

Outside, the sun danced over the heads of the animals and climbed slowly down the sky. "Maybe I can throw this dog away and George won't know," Lennie said. "Then I can feed the rabbits on the farm."

"Do you think about that all the time?" Curley's wife demanded. "Your farm and—rabbits? Why do you like rabbits?"

Lennie moved next to her. He thought about his answer. His leg touched her leg. "I like petting soft, pretty things," he said. "Sometimes I pet mice."

Curley's wife moved away from him a little. "I think you're crazy."

"No, I'm not," Lennie said. "George says I'm not. I like petting nice, soft things with my fingers."

Curley's wife thought about that. "Everybody likes that," she said. "I like beautiful soft clothes. Do you like soft clothes?"

Lennie laughed. "Of course," he cried happily. "My Aunt Clara gave me some nice soft clothes. But I lost them," he remembered sadly.

"You're crazy," Curley's wife said. "But you're a nice man. You're a big baby." She moved her fingers to the top of her head. "Sometimes I like to feel my hair. It's nice and soft. Feel right here."

Lennie felt her hair. "That's really nice," he said. He started

34

to move his hand on her head harder and harder. "That's wonderful."

"Stop now," Curley's wife said. She tried to move her head away but Lennie's fingers closed on her hair. "Stop it! Stop it! You're hurting me," she cried loudly.

But Lennie was scared now and he couldn't stop. He put his hands over her mouth and nose. "Be quiet! Be quiet! George'll be angry. I want to feed the rabbits and work on the farm."

Curley's wife tried to shout.

"Please stop. Stop," Lennie said. Then he was angry with her. "Don't shout. I'll be in trouble. Stop it!" He shook her hard.

Suddenly, her body stopped moving.

Lennie looked down at her and carefully moved his hands away from her mouth. "I don't want to hurt you," he said.

When she didn't answer, he looked at her carefully. He touched her face and arms, but she didn't move. Then he understood. He moved away from the dead woman.

"I did a bad thing. I did another bad thing," he cried. "George will be angry with me. What can I do? They'll come after us. 'The woods,' George said. 'Wait for me in the woods.' "

Chapter 11   The End of It All

The green pool of the Salinas River was beautiful in the late afternoon. Lennie sat down and drank some water.

"George will be angry," he thought. "He'll want to be alone again. I'll go away and leave him alone. I can't feed the rabbits now."

Lennie thought sadly about the animals on the farm. "He won't leave me. George will stay with me. I know George," he cried out loudly to the animals and the trees.

Lennie touched her face and arms, but she didn't move.

George walked slowly out of the woods. "Why are you shouting?" he asked quietly.

"Are you leaving me, George?" Lennie asked.

"No," George said.

"I knew it," Lennie said. "You're my friend. George, I did another bad thing."

"I know."

"Aren't you angry with me?" Lennie asked. "I can go away."

"No," George answered. "You'll always stay with me. We're a family, Lennie."

"We're a family," Lennie repeated excitedly.

George took off his hat. "Take off your hat, Lennie. It's nice and warm."

The big man took off his hat and put it on the ground. "Tell me about the farm, George," he said.

"Look across the river, Lennie, so I can tell you," George said.

Lennie turned his head and looked across the river.

"We'll have a nice little farm ..." George started to tell the story. From his coat, he pulled Carlson's gun. He looked at the back of Lennie's head.

Up the river, a man called and another man answered. Curley and the men were on their way.

"Don't stop. Tell me the story," Lennie repeated.

"We'll have some animals. We'll have chickens and dogs and rabbits," George said.

"And I'll feed the rabbits."

"And you'll feed the rabbits," George said. "Look down the river, Lennie. Can you see the place? We'll have everything and we'll be happy. You and me, Lennie."

"And we'll live off the fat of the land," Lennie said happily.

"Yes, we'll live off the fat of the land."

"Aren't you angry at me, George?" Lennie asked again. "I did a bad thing."

"No, Lennie. I'm not angry."

The sound of the other men was very near now. George looked through the trees and saw their guns.

"Let's buy that farm today," Lennie said.

George put the gun near the back of Lennie's head. "OK, Lennie," he answered. "We won't wait another day. We'll buy the farm now."

The noise of the gun ran up the mountains and back down again. Lennie's body shook and then fell to the ground.

George looked at the gun in his hand and then threw it away from him into the woods.

From the trees, Slim shouted, "George! Where are you, George?"

But George didn't say a word.

ACTIVITIES

Chapters 1–2

Before you read

1 Discuss these questions.
  a Do you have a best friend? How do you help your friend? What does your friend do for you?
  b Do you have a plan for the future? What do you have to do before it happens? Will it be easy?
2 Look at the pictures in the book. What do you think?
  a Are these people in the town or in the country? How do you know?
  b Are these people rich? How do you know?
  c What happened to the dog in the picture on page 33?
  d What is happening to the woman in the picture on page 36?
3 Look at the Word List at the back of the book. Find new words in your dictionary. Put one word in each of these sentences.
  a There is often ..... at football games.
  b The baby is hungry, so I am going to ..... her now.
  c Your coat feels very ..... .
  d The dog ..... the cat from the yard yesterday.
4 Look again at the words in the Word List. Which are words for:
  a animals?
  b a person?
  c a kind of food?
  d a building?
  e a feeling?

While you read

5 Are these sentences right (✓) or wrong (✗)?

   a Lennie is small, dark, and thin.   .....

   b George is tall, wide, and slow.   .....

   c The river water is clean.   .....

   d Lennie remembers everything.   .....

   e Lennie has a dead mouse.   .....

   f The two men are going to work in town.   .....

   g They had problems in Weed.   .....

   h Lennie's second mouse is dead.   .....

   i George has to stay with Lennie.   .....

   j They want to buy a farm.   .....

After you read

6 Who is speaking? What are they talking about?

   a "I don't have mine. I lost it."

   b "OK, George. I'll be quiet. I understand."

   c "They looked for us, but they didn't find us."

   d "I only petted it."

   e "You know the story, so you tell it."

Chapters 3–5

Before you read

7 Look at the names of Chapters 3–5 and at the pictures in those
   chapters. Discuss these questions. What do you think?

   a Who lives in a bunkhouse? What do they do there?

   b Why is the woman dangerous?

   c What is going to happen on the farm?

8 Who are these people?

  a a short, fat man   ....

  b a really hard worker   ....

  c a thin, angry young man   ....

  d a pretty little woman   ....

  e a tall man with black hair   ....

  f a strong man with a large stomach   ....

9 Write one word in each sentence.

  a Lennie is happy because he has a .... from Slim.

  b George started to help Lennie after Lennie's .... died.

  c Then men in Weed were angry because Lennie .... a woman's dress.

  d The puppy is only one .... old.

After you read

10 Discuss these questions. What do you think?

  a Does George take Lennie's money?

  b Is Curley dangerous?

  c Is Lennie dangerous?

  d What does the problem in Weed tell us about Lennie?

  e Does Lennie want to hurt the puppy? Will he?

  f Can Lennie live alone? Why (not)?

11 Work with another student. Have this conversation.

  Student A: You are Lennie. Last night you had to leave Weed. You liked your life there and you don't understand the problem. Ask George questions.

  Student B: You are George. Answer Lennie's questions.

Chapters 6–8

Before you read

12 Discuss these questions. What do you think?

    a Do Lennie and George want to stay on the farm? Why (not)?

    b What is their plan? Is it possible?

While you read

13 Who is speaking? Write the name.

    a "The land will give us everything."

    b "They don't want me here."

    c "A man has to have a good time sometimes."

    d "I don't like fighting."

    e "I'm not interested in your wife."

    f "Hit him!"

    g "Nobody gets any land."

After you read

14 Answer these questions.

    a How are George and Lennie going to get $450?

    b Why is Curley angry with Slim?

    c Why does Lennie hit Curley?

    d Why does Crooks live in a room away from the other men?

    e Why does Lennie visit Crooks?

15 Which of these things do George and Lennie really want to do?

    a make money

    b buy a farm

    c fight with Curley

Chapters 9–11

Before you read

16 What is going to happen? How will the story end? Will George and Lennie have a farm? What do you think?

17 Who is in Crooks's room in Chapter 9? Write the names.

....

....

....

....

18 What happens first? What happens next? Write the numbers, 1–10.

a Curley's wife talks to Lennie. .....

b Lennie is angry with Curley's wife. .....

c Lennie's puppy dies. .....

d Lennie touches Curley's wife's hair. .....

e Lennie shakes Curley's wife. .....

f Lennie waits near the river. .....

g George throws away the gun. .....

h George shoots Lennie. .....

i Curley's wife dies. .....

j Curley's wife tries to shout. .....

After you read

19 Who is Curley's wife talking to? Why does she say these things:

a "Do you think I like being in that house alone?"

b "What happened to your face?"

c "I like machines."

d "Sometimes I want to hurt him, too."

e "I wanted to be in the movies…"

f "You're a big baby."

20 Discuss these questions. What do you think?

a Why don't the men want to talk to Curley's wife? Are they right?

b Why does Lennie throw his puppy on the ground? How does he feel?

c Why does Lennie hurt animals and people?

d Why does George shoot Lennie? How does he feel?

21 Work with another student. Have this conversation.

Student A: You don't know this book but you are interested in it. Is it a good book? Will you enjoy it? Will your father like it? Will your little sister like it? Ask questions about the book.

Student B: You read this book. Answer your friend's questions. Ask him about his father and his sister. What kind of stories do they like?

Writing

22 Write about George and Lennie's plan for the future. What did they want? Was it possible before Curley's wife died?

23 Write about Lennie. What did he like to do? What did he want? Was he a good person or was he a bad person? Why?

24 Write about Curley's wife for the town's newspaper. Where did she come from? How did she die? Who killed her? What happened to her killer? How is Curley now?

25 Write about one of the pictures in the book. Who can you see? What can you see? What is happening?

26 Who in the story did you like? Why? Write about that person.

27 Who in the story did you not like? Why? Write about that person.

28 Write a letter from George to Aunt Clara's daughter. What happened to Lennie? How did you try to stop it? Tell her.

29 Write about your plans for the future. What are they? Do you think they will happen? Why (not)?

Answers for the Activities in this book are available from the Penguin Readers website. A free Activity Worksheet is also available from the website. Activity Worksheets are part of the Penguin Teacher Support Programme, which also includes Progress Tests and Graded Reader Guidelines. For more information, please visit: www.penguinreaders.com.

WORD LIST *with example sentences*

alone (adj/adv) After everybody left, I was *alone* in the house.

bastard (n) Did you hit that child, you *bastard*?

body (n) He washed his face and *body* in the river.

bunkhouse (n) The farm workers sleep in a *bunkhouse*, but they eat with us in the farmhouse.

chase (v) The dogs *chased* the cat out of the yard.

crush (v) He *crushed* the can in his hand and threw it on the ground.

demand (v) I *demand* an answer to my question—now!

feed (v) Who is going to *feed* the chickens this morning?

ketchup (n) They can't eat hamburgers without *ketchup*.

land (n) We are going to buy a house with a lot of *land*.

live off the fat of the land They worked hard on the farm for ten years, and after that they *lived off the fat of the land*.

mouse (n) I hear *mice* in the kitchen at night, but I never see them.

pet (v) Don't *pet* strange dogs! Some dogs are dangerous.

puppy (n) The dog was happier after her *puppies* were born.

rabbit (n) Last year *rabbits* ate the vegetables in our yard.

scared (adj) I'm *scared* in an empty house at night.

shake (v) He woke up when she *shook* his arm.

soft (adj) These clothes are very *soft*. What do you use when you wash them?

touch (v) Don't *touch* the glass! You'll cut your hand.

trouble (n) After strangers arrived at the party, there was *trouble*.

A Christmas Carol

Charles Dickens

Scrooge is a cold, hard man. He loves money, and he doesn't like people. He really doesn't like Christmas. But then some ghosts visit him. They show him his past life, his life now, and a possible future. Will Scrooge learn from the ghosts? Can he change?

Rain Man

Charlie Babbitt thinks he will inherit his father's money. But the money goes to a man with autism – the brother Charlie never knew he had. So starts a surprising new life for both of them. *Also a major film starring Tom Cruise and Dustin Hoffman.*

Robin Hood

Robin Hood robbed rich people and gave the money to the poor. He fought against the greedy Sheriff of Nottingham and bad Prince John and defended the beautiful Lady Marian. *Robin Hood is a folk-hero and the story is supposed to be true!*

There are hundreds of Penguin Readers to choose from – world classics, film adaptations, modern-day crime and adventure, short stories, biographies, American classics, non-fiction, plays ...

For a complete list of all Penguin Readers titles, please contact your local Pearson Longman office or visit our website.

www.penguinreaders.com

Braveheart
Randall Wallace

Braveheart is the true story of William Wallace who led his people to fight for Scotland, the country they loved. *Braveheart is an exhilarating and moving film directed by and starring Mel Gibson.*

The Prince and the Pauper
Mark Twain

Two babies are born on the same day in England. One boy is a prince and the other boy is from a very poor family. Ten years later, they change places for a game. But then the old king dies and they cannot change back. Will the poor boy be the new King of England?

Forrest Gump
Winston Groom

A warm tale of a good-hearted young man from Alabama, who wins a medal for bravery in the Vietnam War and meets the President. *An Oscar-winning film starring Tom Hanks.*

There are hundreds of Penguin Readers to choose from – world classics, film adaptations, modern-day crime and adventure, short stories, biographies, American classics, non-fiction, plays ...

For a complete list of all Penguin Readers titles, please contact your local Pearson Longman office or visit our website.

www.penguinreaders.com

Gandhi
Jane Rollason

Mahatma Gandhi was one of the most important and influential people of the twentieth century. His message of peaceful resistance changed the world. This lively biography explains how.

How to be an Alien
George Mikes

How to be an Alien is the funniest book you will read about the English! Why are the English different from Europeans? George Mikes' book describes the strange things the English do and say. And because the English are strange, they don't get angry when they read the book. They love it! You will too!

My Fair Lady

Eliza Doolittle is a poor flower-seller with a strong London accent. Professor Higgins wants to teach her to speak like a lady but things don't happen as he plans. *Based on Pygmalion by George Bernard Shaw and made into a musical film starring Audrey Hepburn.*

There are hundreds of Penguin Readers to choose from – world classics, film adaptations, modern-day crime and adventure, short stories, biographies, American classics, non-fiction, plays ...

For a complete list of all Penguin Readers titles, please contact your local Pearson Longman office or visit our website.

www.penguinreaders.com

Longman Dictionaries

Express yourself with confidence!

Longman has led the way in ELT dictionaries since 1935.
We constantly talk to students and teachers around the
world to find out what they need from a learner's dictionary.

Why choose a *Longman dictionary?*

Easy to understand

Longman invented the Defining Vocabulary – 2000 of the most common words which are used to write the definitions in our dictionaries. So Longman definitions are always clear and easy to understand.

Real, natural English

All Longman dictionaries contain natural examples taken from real-life that help explain the meaning of a word and show you how to use it in context.

Avoid common mistakes

Longman dictionaries are written specially for learners, and we make sure that you get all the help you need to avoid common mistakes. We analyse typical learners' mistakes and include notes on how to avoid them.

Innovative CD-ROMs

Longman are leaders in dictionary CD-ROM innovation. Did you know that a dictionary CD-ROM includes features to help improve your pronunciation, help you practice for exams and improve your writing skills?

For details of all Longman dictionaries, and to choose
the one that's right for you, visit our website:

www.longman.com/dictionaries